SO YOU WANT TO BE A VIKING?

Written by
GEORGIA AMSON-BRADSHAW

Illustrated by
TAKAYO AKIYAMA

Inspired by the book *Viking* by
JOHN HAYWOOD

Thames & Hudson

So you want to be a Viking?
© 2019 Thames & Hudson Ltd, London

Based on the book by John Haywood
Viking © 2011 Thames & Hudson Ltd, London

Illustrations © 2019 Takayo Akiyama

Abridged from the original by Georgia Amson-Bradshaw
Designed by Belinda Webster

First published in 2019 in hardcover in the United States of America by
Thames & Hudson Inc., 500 Fifth Avenue, New York, New York 10110

www.thamesandhudsonusa.com

Library of Congress Control Number 2019931890

ISBN 978-0-500-65184-1

Printed and bound in China by Everbest Printing Co. Ltd

7

WHERE TO START?

So you want to be a VIKING? 10

Bjorn's Viking CHECKLIST 12

Which LEADER should you follow? 16

Choose your WEAPONS 28

Shopping for your GEAR 32

Getting ship-shape 36

SHIPWRECK! 42

If sailing isn't for you... 46

Become a BESERKER 48

5 epic places to PLUNDER   50

Hervor's CAMPAIGN pep talk   58

Get ready to CHARGE!   70

The BOOTY   76

The SWORD'S sleep   84

Viking world MAP   88

Glossary   90

Reading RUNES   93

Index   94

SO YOU WANT TO BE A ...
VIKING?

I'm Sigurd the Skald*
and I sing of brave deeds,
adventures and battles,
so young ones take heed.

To become Viking warriors
it's courage you'll need,
but you'll go down in
history if you succeed!

I'm as brave as
they come, Sigurd!

*A skald is a poet,
who does know it.

Big-headed as they
come, more like.

THE VIKING SING-A-LONG

The life of a VIKING may be rather GORY,
But RISK is rewarded with RICHES and GLORY.

You'll have GOLD COINS and JEWELS,
FURS and FINE CLOTHES.

There'll be SONGS sung about you
that everyone knows.

To join up you need to have SKILLS
and GOOD BREEDING.

To see if you meet the requirements,
KEEP READING...

Furs and fine clothes?
Viking life sounds fancy!

I'm Bjorn, the strongest Viking warrior in history. People often think everyone in Scandinavia is a Viking. But actually, only warrior kings, or incredible fighters like me, are lucky enough to make it their full-time job.

VIKING CHECKLIST

Check all boxes that apply

1. I AM A KING

You don't need a kingdom to be called a king in Scandinavia, you just need an army. To have (and hold on to) a Viking army, you need to be rich enough to pay soldiers to fight for you.

Don't worry about inheriting a throne either. You can always invade a country and set up your very own throne and surrounding kingdom there.

2. I AM POSH

The next level below the king is the JARLS. The jarls are a bit like dukes, and are always trying to increase their wealth and status. Leading raids is a good way for a jarl to climb the ranks.

$$$

I'll buy the more expensive one. Just because I can.

3. I AM ARMED

Even if you aren't posh, you can still volunteer as a Viking if you are a freeman (not owned by someone) and have your own weapons.

I'm armed and dangerous

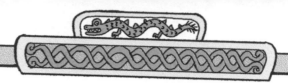

4. I AM A WARRIOR WOMAN

Most women join Viking raids as camp followers, doing the cooking, washing and sewing. But a few of the very bravest noblewomen are known to have become Viking warriors as well as high-ranking officers who decide on tactics and strategy.

I decide the strateg you two do what I say!

My name is Hervor. Heroic women warriors like me are called **SHIELD-MAIDENS** and we appear in a lot of Viking sagas (myths and legends). I took my father's sword from his grave and became a seafaring raider. As it turns out the sword is cursed...

5. I AM CRAFTY

Even if you don't actually become a Viking and go fighting, you can still join a raid if you have a craft or trade. Ships and weapons always need fixing, and traders help Vikings sell their captured slaves, or thralls, and stolen goods for hard cash.

How much will you give me for this one?

Hey, I'm with you guys!

NOT ELIGIBLE

If you are a thrall, bad luck—you can't become a Viking. But that doesn't mean you can avoid the risk of violent death. You may still be made to fight as part of your owner's blood feud with a neighbor. Not fair!

Um, do you think you might be over-reacting.

That Viking gave me a funny look. Go and kill him for me!

An eager young warrior with hunger and nerve must first choose which Viking leader to serve. Do you favor courage or cunning or skill? Choose wisely—poor leaders will get you all killed.

WHICH
VIKING LEADER SHOULD YOU FOLLOW?

1. CHOOSE A SPECIAL ABILITY

A

expert at building fortifications

B

has a big family to fight for him

C

very agile, can juggle knives

D

has skalds to write stories

2. CHOOSE YOUR FIGHTER

A

cunning

B

brave

C

merciless

D

violent

3. PICK A PERSONALITY TRAIT

A

old and
experienced

B

scary and
wild-looking

C

young and
ambitious

D

royal and
well-connected

4. WHERE DO YOU WANT TO RAID?

A

England

B

Mediterranean

C

Scandinavia

D

Ireland

OUNT UP YOUR A, B, C AND D ANSWERS. CHECK THE RESULTS ON THE NEXT PAGE >>>

QUIZ RESULTS:

IF YOU CHOSE **MOSTLY A's**
FOLLOW: HASTEIN

The son of a Danish peasant farmer, Hastein's cunning has made him one of the greatest Vikings of all time. On one raid, he tricked the townspeople of Luna, Italy, by pretending to be dead. His warriors asked to give their dead chief a Christian burial inside the town. The locals agreed and when Hastein's Vikings carried him into the town in a coffin, he leapt out, killed the bishop and looted the city. He has carried out many successful raids in England.

MOSTLY B's
RAGNAR LODBROK

Ragnar has had three wives, and has enough sons to make up a longship crew. He wears shaggy trousers—which give him a wild look and earned him the nickname "Hairy Breeches." He is famous for his bravery in killing two giant snakes in Sweden.

MOSTLY C's
OLAF TRYGGVASON

Olaf learned about being a Viking the hard way. As a baby prince, the ship he was sailing on was captured by the Viking Klerkon who took baby Olaf to be his thrall. When Olaf was 8, his cousin Sigurd found him and bought his freedom. Aged 9, Olaf spotted Klerkon in the market, and killed him with an axe. Since then, he has continued to prove himself a merciless and fearsome warrior.

MOSTLY D's
ERIK BLOODAXE

Son of Harald Fairhair, the king who united Norway, Erik Bloodaxe went on his first raid aged 12. After his father died, he became joint king with two of his brothers, but he wasn't keen on sharing so he killed them. He started to kill his subjects, too, until they kicked him out of Norway. He is not the best Viking but his skalds are skilled at writing so he is very famous as a result.

ALL ABOARD
THE LONGSHIP

Welcome to our Viking army! I'm Bjorn, your leader on today's raid. Please make sure your helmets are on tight and all swords are stowed away in their sheaths before we take off.

In the event of an emergency, do not attempt to exit or your honor will be stripped away from you. Have a safe raid!

MEET YOUR CREW

The crew of a single longship can be considered an army in Viking terms. To invade another country, a lot of small armies will band together. These raiding armies might number 5,000 or 6,000 warriors.

HONOR AND OBEY

There's no formal discipline in a Viking army, because it isn't needed. Honor is what keeps everyone in their place. If a Viking runs away from battle, he loses all his honor. After that he will be kicked out of his village, considered legally dead and all his property will be destroyed or given away.

BORN BATTLE READY

Viking armies don't really do training. Your parents are responsible for teaching you basic weapon skills. Luckily for me, my loving parents taught me how to fight and kill from a very young age!

BABY'S FIRST AXE

Here's me being given my first weapon. Vikings give their children toy swords as soon as they can walk. If your family is rich enough, they will probably give you your first iron weapons when you are about 10 years old.

FIELD DAY

Here's me winning gold in archery. Competitive sports are a great way to develop the skills a warrior needs. We encourage aggression and violent behavior in all our youngsters.

GRADUATION

And here's a picture of me on my first day in the defense force. For poor kids, the defense force is often their first bit of battle training.

HERVOR'S GUIDE
HOW TO FIT IN WITH YOUR SQUAD

> LISTEN UP, LOSERS.
> To be a full-time warrior, you have to join the private army of a king or jarl. You don't want to look like a noob. Here's how to blend in.

RULES FOR NEW VIKINGS

TIP #1

Obey the rules. When you first join a Viking army, you'll have to swear an oath to obey the squad rules. If you break the rules, you'll be thrown off the squad!

NEVER BETRAY YOUR CHIEF. SERIOUSLY, DON'T DO IT.

BJORN 4 EVA

NO FIGHTING ANYONE IN YOUR SQUAD— STAY CHILL, OK?

IF YOU COME ACROSS SOMEONE WHO HAS BEEN BANISHED FROM THE SQUAD FOR BREAKING ONE OF THESE RULES, **THEY MUST DIE.**

TIME TO DIE

TIP #2

Everyone in the squad lives in the king's or jarl's house. You all sleep together in the hall (except the king who gets a private bedroom). TOP VIKINGS get to sit near the king at the feast table. LOSERS are stuck down the other end. Do whatever you can to sit close to the king.

Kings and jarls hold feasts to show off how powerful and rich they are. There's always a lot of boiled or roasted meat and blood sausage, so it's too bad if you're vegetarian.

TIP #3

Vikings care a lot about their reputations, so make sure you loudly boast about your brave deeds to boost your cred.

Don't push it, though—if your boasts are too ridiculous, you'll look like an idiot. And DON'T boast that you're going to do something super-dangerous—people will remember and hold you to it...

TIP #4

Unfortunately, if someone insults you, you're not allowed to kill them there and then. Instead you must challenge them to a duel inside a marked-out area. At that point, you can legally kill them, OR if they place one foot outside the dueling area, they "yield" and have to pay you money. You can make pretty good money by challenging feeble fighters to duels.

VIOLETS ARE BLUE,

ROSES ARE RED,

YOU SMELL LIKE FARTS

AND YOU'RE SOFT
IN THE HEAD.

TIP #5

A less violent way to restore your honor is to write a rude poem about your opponent. If it's catchy enough, people will remember it and it will ruin your enemy's reputation. You could even challenge them to a face-to-face exchange of insults at a feast, kind of like a rap battle. The audience decides who wins.

CHOOSE YOUR WEAPONS

Getting a full set of gear will cost you a lot of cash. Luckily, you can join a raid even if you only have the basics.

SPEAR
Most warriors start out with a spear, and unless they get rich they might never get to fight with anything else. Viking spears have an ash-wood shaft around 6.5-8 ft long, and a metal blade.

SHIELD
You'll get through several shields on a campaign because they get smashed to pieces. Viking shields are wooden and round, and although you don't have to paint yours, having a unique shield design will make sure your brave deeds in battle are noticed. This will encourage skalds to write poems about you.

EDDIE THE UNBREAKABLE

Great, Eddie! As long as your shield doesn't bre

AXE

When most people think of Vikings, they think of axes. Axes are cheaper to make than swords because they use less iron. But they are still extremely effective at removing your enemies' limbs. There are small handaxes for fighting at close quarters, and huge broadaxes that can chop down anyone within a 6.5 ft radius.

BOW

In situations where it's hard to get close to your enemy, such as a sea battle or a castle siege, a bow is a handy weapon. They also double up as something to catch your dinner with.

(but good luck catching rabbits with a battleaxe)

SWORD

The weapon that every Viking really wants is a sword. It might take a blacksmith more than a year to make a single sword, so they cost a lot of money.

If you're lucky enough to be born into a rich family, or successful enough (like me!) to save up, here's what you need to look for in a sword:

TOP TIP
If you think you're being smart by stealing your dead father's sword, think again. This cursed sword gives me nothing but grief.

That's not the hairstyle I had in mind.

✔ The BLADE should be 25–30 inches long. A shorter sword is easier to handle, but a longer sword causes more damage

✘ There shouldn't be any rust or pit marks on the blade (these are signs of poor-quality iron).

✔ The HILT (handle) balances the weight of the blade when you hold it. A poorly balanced sword will tire out your arm.

BLING UP YOUR SWORD

Once you've bought a blade, you can add things to your sword to make it look extra blingy.

Set a **MAGIC HEALING STONE** in the hilt. Any wound made by the sword won't heal unless it is touched by the stone.

DECORATE the hilt and scabbard with blingy gold and silver.

Emboss **MAGIC RUNES** on the blade to give you protection in battle.

CAUTION
It's tempting to use something shiny like gold for the handgrip, but it's a bad idea. Rough cord is ugly but it stops your hand from slipping from sweat or blood in battle.

Give your sword a **FLASHY NAME** to pump up its reputation. Something like Giantslayer or Demonblade.

SHOPPING FOR YOUR GEAR

If you can afford it, buy some armor.
It looks good and keeps you in one piece.
It might cost an arm and a leg, but it will literally save
you an arm and a leg. Here's what it will cost you:

PRICES
(IN WEIGHT OF SILVER)

★ SPEAR - 1.5 OZ

★ HELMET - 15 OZ

★ MAIL SHIRT - 25 OZ

★ SWORD - UP TO 3.7 LB

Can I pay the rest when I get my allowance?

HELMET

Most Vikings don't wear helmets because they're expensive.
They just wear a padded leather cap, or nothing at all.
If you can afford a helmet, it will be a simple conical
shape. And as every wannabe Viking knows:

Why are you dressed like a cow?

Viking helmets do **NOT** have horns!

Ooh, a vintage mail shirt, gorgeous!

MAIL SHIRT

Vikings wear mail, rather
than plate armor. A single mail
shirt might be made of 30,000
metal rings welded together,
and can weigh 25 lb. It's a good
idea to wear a tight belt so
that some of the weight rests
on your hips, instead of your
shoulders.

SUPER SKILLS

Vikings aren't famous for using fancy battle formations like the Romans. They are famous for being incredibly tough. Even so, there are a few top battle techniques that you'll want to have in your skill set.

SHIELD WALL

This classic move isn't complicated. You all line up so that your shields overlap, like a wall. Ideally there are about four rows of Vikings lined up, all pushing forward to break the enemy's line.

I don't know who I'm more scared of who's behind or who's in front.

Any time a warrior falls, someone from the row behind can move forward to take their place.

SWINE-WEDGE

According to folklore, this move was invented by the god of war, Odin. Everyone lines up to make a wedge shape, so that all the pushing force is focused on a small part of the enemy's line. A wedge is the same shape as a swine's head.

I said "swine-wedge" not "swine-wedgie"!

SHIELD-BURG

An upgraded shield wall, the shield-burg also protects against missiles from above. The warriors in the middle hold their shields up above their heads to create a roof. This is useful when attacking the walls of a city or fort.

GETTING SHIP-SHAPE

Scandinavia is mostly surrounded by sea, so there's a lot of sailing involved in being a Viking. Two types of longships are used for battles: drakkars and snekkes. You'll need to be familiar with them and how to sail them.

STERN

SAIL

GUNWHALE

STEERING OAR

OARS

Ha! That drakkar is the spitting image of my uncle Arthur.

36

DRAKKARS

Drakkars, or "dragons", are huge, fancy longships. They are very expensive, and only owned by kings or jarls. They can be up to 118 feet long, with 80 oarsmen, and can transport as many as 500 warriors on a short trip. In a sea battle, a single drakkar can take on five or six snekkes.

MAST

ROPES

FIGUREHEAD

TRESTLES

PROW

HULL

SNEKKES

Snekkes, or "snakes", are very narrow warships about 55-70 feet long. This makes them very fast, and because their hulls are shallow, they can be sailed up quite small rivers without running aground. They need 24-36 oarsmen to row them, and are excellent for the quick hit-and-run raids called strandhogg.

The Vikings are coming in snakes!

What beautiful weather for being on the water.

TOP TIP:
Salt water rusts iron very quickly so grease your weapons and armor before you sail.

LIFE ON BOARD

In good weather, being on a Viking ship is quite pleasant. In bad weather, it's a different story. The deck is completely open and can't be covered with hides or blankets because they act like sails and make the ship hard to steer. Fires can't be lit on board. So expect to be freezing, wet and very seasick.

FINDING YOUR WAY

Vikings sail great distances in search of loot and adventure. Some have even sailed all the way from Scandinavia to Canada! If you learn the same navigational skills, you too can sail around the world.

POSITION OF THE SUN

In the northern hemisphere, the sun is due south at midday. Its height helps you guess how far north you are. The higher the sun is in the sky at midday, the further south you are. But don't look directly at the sun— or you won't be able to see anything anymore.

SUN STONE

What do you do if it's cloudy and you can't see the sun? It's thought that Viking navigators used a sun stone. This is a clear crystal that changes color when held up to the sky and pointed in the direction of the sun.

BIRD WATCHING

During the summer, sea birds fly out in the morning to feed on fish, and return to feed their chicks in the evening. Some types of sea bird will fly further out to sea than others. By paying attention to the type of birds you can see, and the direction they are flying, you can get an idea of where land is.

FOLLOW THE COAST

Where possible, the easiest thing to do is simply sail along the coast, keeping landmarks in sight. To sail from Denmark to England, for example, it's safest to sail down the coast to Belgium, cross the English Channel, then sail up the English coast to wherever you're going.

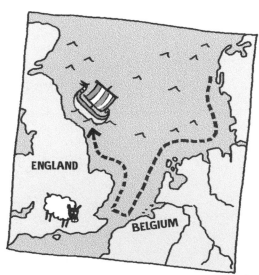

SHIPWRECK!

Sometimes even the best sailors get into trouble. If you find yourself caught in a storm, here's what to do:

HOLD ON TIGHT

If you are in the open ocean, and the waves aren't too high, your best bet is to lower the sails, let the ship drift and hold on tight.

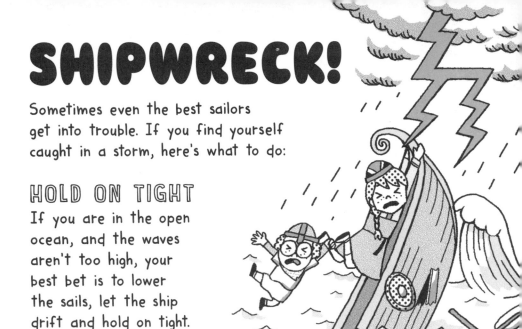

HEAD FOR LAND

The danger of drifting is that, if you are near land, your ship might be driven onto the shore and wrecked. So it's best to sail straight for the land, but even this is dangerous because if you misjudge it the ship might turn to the side and crash against the rocks.

So that's where the coast is.

PREVENTATIVE MEASURES

It's better to try to prevent a shipwreck from happening in the first place by using magic. Get an expert to carve protective runes onto the ship. Many storms are caused by bad spirits, so a scary figurehead will frighten them off.

UNTYING ONE KNOT GIVES YOU A BREEZE

UNTYING TWO KNOTS BRINGS A STRONG WIND

UNTYING THREE KNOTS CAUSES A TERRIBLE GALE

BUYING WIND

Wizards from Finland can sell you magic knotted ropes that provide wind if you find yourself stuck at sea. Untying one knot gives you a breeze, untying two knots brings a strong wind and untying three knots causes a terrible gale.

FOUR-LEGGED TRANSPORT

Unless you only plan on raiding cities on the coast, you're going to need to travel overland as well as over water. Speed is important when raiding, so walking is too slow. You need horses.

BRING YOUR OWN

If you're only sailing a short distance, one option is to take your horses with you. However, horses make terrible sailors— they don't row and they take up a lot of space.

Can you budge a little?

A FREE RIDE

A better plan, especially if you're sailing far, is to get horses when you arrive. The locals will usually be happy to "donate" their horses to you if they think it means you'll ride off and leave them alone.

TREASURE MULE

Horses are also very useful once you've finished raiding. After all, hopefully you will have acquired a lot of heavy baggage along the way (treasure isn't light).

If you really want to be a Viking but sailing isn't for you...

JOIN THE VARANGIAN GUARD

This is an army of Viking troops working for the Byzantine emperor Basil in Mikligard (modern-day Istanbul).

SOLDIERS FOR HIRE

It's not unusual for Vikings to work as mercenaries (soldiers for hire), but Basil has taken this a step further, creating a special Viking-only unit. He thinks that, as foreigners, Vikings are less likely to get involved in local politics or be disloyal.

VIKINGS FOR HIRE

LOYAL. BLOODTHIRSTY. SCARY. WILL MEET ALL YOUR VIOLENT ENTERTAINMENT NEEDS.

PAY TO WORK, WORK TO PLAY

It costs several pounds of gold to join the VARANGIAN GUARD. It might seem weird to pay to get a job, but this means it's only rich Vikings who are able to join.

Once in the Guard, Vikings can earn a basic pay of 2 lbs of gold per year, along with a big share of any loot from war and raids, and frequent gifts from the emperor. As a result, the entrance fee is soon recovered.

THE KEY DUTIES OF THE
VARANGIAN GUARD
✔ protecting the emperor
✔ killing traitors
✔ fighting alongside the emperor
✔ catching pirates in the navy.

In their downtime, they can:
✔ watch chariot races
✔ rest in their top-quality accommodation
✔ get very drunk.

If discipline isn't really your thing...

BECOME A BERSERKER

Do you have a habit of flying into a violent and uncontrollable rage over the smallest things? You might be in luck! It could be that Odin, the god of war, has gifted you with the special powers needed to become a berserker.

I bless you with very poor anger-management skills

AR&*&URGH!!!*!&

FEEL NO PAIN

Berserkers perform secret rituals together before battle to work themselves up into a terrifying trance-like rage. In their trances they howl like wild animals and bite their shields, and are completely immune to pain.

PSYCHOLOGICAL WARFARE

Because they feel no pain, berserkers don't bother wearing armor, and instead just wear bear or wolf skins. This has the added benefit of freaking out the enemy. Being faced with a howling opponent who doesn't care at all for their safety has a powerful psychological effect.

Whose idea was it to fight the Vikings again?

FRIENDLY FIRE

Unfortunately, berserkers aren't only dangerous to the enemy. They are prone to flying into uncontrollable rages and can kill or injure several people on their own side before they calm down. Because of this, there aren't many working in armies, and they often end up as outlaws.

What happened?

He called Ulf a fifl —it means idiot.

49

BEST DESTINATIONS

When you are planning a raid, take a moment to consider: How long is the journey? What sort of enemies will I encounter? Which types of booty are there for the taking? This will help you to choose your destination.

BLOODY PLANET

5 EPIC PLACES TO PLUNDER
BEFORE YOU DIE
(VIOLENTLY)

FINLAND

The snowy lands to the north are great for picking up some fashionable fur and trying out winter sports.

★ ★ ★
LOCATION: North
BEST BOOTY: Furs, walrus ivory

The **SKI-FINNS** are nomadic, meaning they never stop traveling. They move over the snow on skis, following reindeer herds. In winter they hunt bears and reindeer, and trap otters, foxes and squirrels for meat and fur. In summer they hunt seals for their skins, and walrus for their ivory teeth.

★ TOP TIP

Watch out for the Ski-Finns' powerful **BOWS**. In winter they are especially deadly, launching surprise arrow attacks, then whizzing away on their skis. They also have witches who use powerful black magic to bring storms.

ENGLAND

This green and pleasant land has got to be at the top of every Viking's bucket list.

★ ★ ★ ★ ★

LOCATION: South-west across the North Sea

BEST BOOTY: Livestock and cash

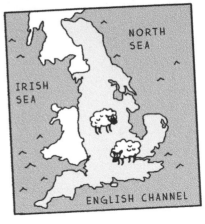

For a long time, England was ruled by tough kings who scared off even the largest Viking armies. But now, weak **KING AETHELRED** is in charge. Make the most of this once-in-a-lifetime opportunity! Nowhere in England is far from the sea, and old Roman roads provide speedy routes across land.

★ TOP TIP

AETHELRED has started paying Viking armies to go away and leave England alone, but this has just attracted more Vikings. Join a big campaign to get your slice of the payoff.

IRELAND

Come for gorgeous scenery
and the friendly people...
then leave with the people too!

★ ★ ★
LOCATION: West of Britain
BEST BOOTY: Thralls

Ireland, especially the
monasteries, have been sacked
repeatedly over the last
200 years. However, the one
thing they still have in great
quantities is people, who can
be captured and sold as thralls.

> We've run out of treasure!

> You'll have to do, then.

★ TOP TIP

In open battle, the Irish don't put up much resistance.
They fight almost naked and have poor-quality weapons.

WENDLAND

Come and visit beautiful, wealthy towns, just a short hop from home.

BALTIC SEA

WENDLAND

★ ★ ★ ★
LOCATION: South, across the Baltic Sea
BEST BOOTY: Silver and amber

Wendland is just a short sea voyage away, making it perfect for a quick summer raid. Wendland has many trading towns on important rivers, so they have a lot of silver. But watch out: those towns are well protected.

Run, run as fast as you can! Can't catch me, I'm a Wends man!

★ TOP TIP

THE WENDS fight on foot and on horseback. They are very skilled at setting ambushes, so be careful when chasing after **WENDS** who look like they are running away—it might be a trap.

SPAIN

Great food awaits the Viking who makes it as far as sunny Spain.

★

LOCATION: South, below Frankia
BEST BOOTY: Food, wine and treasure

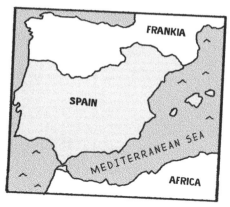

FRANKIA

SPAIN

MEDITERRANEAN SEA

AFRICA

Spain tempts many a Viking traveler in search of the good life—delicious food, sunny weather and cities full of treasure. Unfortunately THE MOORS who rule Spain have an army of excellent warriors to keep Viking hands off all their goodies.

I don't think I like Spain after all!

t's almost impossible to get around
he south coast of Spain because
he narrow gap between Spain and
frica is protected by a MOORISH
eet of ships. But fighting on land
't much easier—THE MOORS
e well armed and well trained.

OTHER PLACES TO VISIT
(BUT NOT TO RAID)

GARDARIKI ★ ★ ★ ★
(RUSSIA)

Across the Eastern Sea is Gardariki, the land of the Rus. The Rus people are descended from Swedish Vikings themselves, so they are friends. You can visit Gardariki to trade your booty for furs, or for silk and spices from further east.

I'll swap you that for a seagull's claw.

FRANKIA ★
(FRANCE)

This fabulous area is full of rich towns and abbeys, with great farmland and easily navigable rivers. Sadly, the window of opportunity for raiding is now closed, as Frankish kings have paid some Vikings to stop other Vikings from plundering. But you're welcome to stop by for some rest and relaxation if you fancy a winter break.

> Is that the sun setting or our ship on fire?

MIKLIGARD ★
(CONSTANTINOPLE)

On the shore of the Black Sea is the stunning city of Mikligard (modern-day Istanbul). It's probably the richest city in the world, but don't let that tempt you to raid it—it's incredibly well defended, and the Greeks have a secret weapon: GREEK FIRE. It's a type of flammable liquid that burns even when floating on water.

If you want to visit Mikligard, you could sign up to the Varangian Guard, or you could simply visit as a tourist and take advantage of the fantastic shopping opportunities. In the markets you'll find merchants selling everything from wine, oil, grain, treasure and silk to thralls.

HERVOR'S CAMPAIGN PEP TALK

You probably think raiding is all about battles and looting. Wrong! Most of the time it's just a lot of sitting around in camp, or marching somewhere in the rain. It's pretty lousy to be honest. Sure you still wanna go?

1. DO YOUR RESEARCH

You don't just want to bust in somewhere without doing your research first. At least TRY to be a bit clever about it. If you're going to a Christian country, find out when their religious festivals are and attack then, when everyone is busy. And don't forget to ask the gods for advice—they can tell you if your plans are good or not.

A SEERESS can speak to the spirits for you after dining on a sacred meal of animal hearts.

2. PACK YOUR RAINCOAT

When you're on campaign you have to be prepared for all kinds of weather—you can't just pop home to dry out and warm up. Get a waterproof cloak to keep the rain out. Sealskin is the best, but if you can't afford it, a greased leather cloak works well too.

3. GET SQUEAKY CLEAN

Vikings might be fierce, but they are always clean and well groomed. In fact, English women are known to prefer the company of Viking men because of their superior style and personal hygiene. Bathe every week, comb your hair every day to keep it free of nits and launder your clothes regularly—even on campaign.

4. STOW AWAY YOUR LOOT

If you're planning on doing a whole season of campaigning somewhere, you'll need to build a fort when you get there. This is to protect the ships and any loot you collect. Pick a sheltered, well-drained place so you don't find yourself sleeping in a puddle.

A simple fort is all you need: a U-shaped dirt bank, open to the river, with a ditch in front and sharp wooden posts on top.

If you're going to be based in the same place for a few years, it's worth forcing the local peasants to build some proper houses and stronger defenses for you.

5. LEARN HOW TO KILL TIME

In between killing people to steal their stuff, there's a lot of sitting around killing time. Ways to keep yourself amused include: chatting, playing games, wrestling and holding archery competitions.

> OK, so Ulf bets three gold pieces.

> !OUH£%KKAAH!!

If you're traveling with a king or jarl, there will probably be a skald with you to ENTERTAIN the warriors.

GAMBLING is another popular pastime. You can bet on dice and board games, horse fights or drinking competitions—anything that's going on. Just try not to gamble away all your loot before you get home.

6. TRY NOT TO STARVE

Vikings are hardy folk, but cold and hunger will still destroy a Viking army. In winter the roads turn into deep, sticky mud, there's no grass for the horses and food is hard to come by. Because of this, most campaigning stops over the winter.

Summer is finally over.

In the summer it's easy to take food from the countryside as you pass through it, but an army of **1,000** warriors needs **2,000 LBS** of bread and **1,000 LBS** of meat every day. Try not to stay over winter where you've already plundered —unless you have good stores of food, the army can starve.

That's today's shopping.

7. HEAD HOME OR HOLE UP

The obvious plan is to head home for the winter with your loot, back to your warm halls and food stores. If you're not going to your own home, another option is to kick some locals out of theirs. Capture an enemy town with ready-built houses and defences to hole up in until the weather gets better.

HERVOR'S TOP TIPS FOR WINTERING ABROAD

1 DON'T STAY IN AN AREA YOU'VE ALREADY RAVAGED. THERE WON'T BE ANY FOOD LEFT IF YOU ATE IT ALL IN SUMMER.

2 RICH LANDOWNERS AND CHURCHES STORE A LOT OF FOOD OVER WINTER. FIND OUT WHERE THEY KEEP IT ALL AND STEAL IT.

3 FORAGING PARTIES GOING OUT FOR FOOD ARE EASY TO ATTACK. MAKE SURE THEY GO IN BIG GROUPS TO DEFEND THEMSELVES.

WINNERS AND LOSERS

A*%R+GH!!

Ulf loves to battle. But unless you are a berserker like Ulf, it's important to consider the possible risks and rewards before rushing in to fight.

RISKS

★ The most obvious risk is that you might LOSE. Then you'll either go home empty-handed, or possibly you won't go home at all.

HERE LIES ULF

★ Even if you don't die, you may need to find a new army to join. Defeat is very bad for a commander's reputation, so warriors will often leave to find a new (better) commander to follow.

REWARDS

★ You might **WIN!** If you do, you'll be in a good position to ask for money from your defeated enemies.

★ If you win, you'll most likely get rich. Victory in Viking battles could earn you enough to buy your own longship and the world.

★ Battle is a chance to prove yourself and build up your reputation. The warrior who fights like a hero is treated like a hero.

VIKING **MINDFULNESS** WITH SIGURD THE SKALD

POEM FOR THE
MINDFUL WARRIOR

There aren't any WORDS that can truly CONVEY
What BATTLE is like in the HEAT of the FRAY.

Before it BEGINS there's a terrible WAIT,
While EVERYONE nervously ponders their FATE.

First both sides exchange ARROWS and SPEARS,
Then the TWO ARMIES begin to draw NEAR.

That makes me feel MORE anxious, Sigurd!

The LINES meet at last, and the shield walls CLASH,
Each FIGHTER starts to hack and to SLASH.

Amidst DEAFENING NOISE, the ground turns to MUD,
With SEVERED LIMBS, spilled GUTS
and fountains of BLOOD.

Soon one side's FIGHTERS will start to FALL FAST,
One way or another, it's over at LAST.

PICK YOUR BATTLEFIELD

Try to choose a spot that will give your army an advantage, and get into position before the battle starts. Once the fighting begins, it'll be too late to get organized.

Pick a brave soldier to be your standard (flag) bearer—they are a prime target for the enemy.

Being on a hill, or having a ditch or river in front of your line gives you a natural advantage. It's much harder for the enemy to attack if they have to cross water or run uphill.

Everyone fights on foot, even the commander. It would be bad for morale if the commander was on a horse, and could escape easily if the going gets tough. Horses are kept at the back, out of the way.

Get ready to rumble!

The commander fights at the front. This inspires the warriors, letting them know the commander faces the same risks that they do.

69

GET READY TO CHARGE!

You've weighed up the risks, prepared yourself mentally and chosen your battlefield. Before the battle starts, try to scare your enemies by putting on a show.

1. POLISH your armour the night before. Dress magnificently, and wave your standards, or flags, triumphantly.

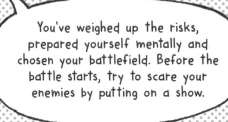

2. PRAY to the gods. It doesn't matter which one, so long as your enemy thinks the gods are on your side.

3. Make lots of NOISE. Shout, scream, beat your shield and blow the war trumpets.

4. Get the BERSERKERS going. Make sure the enemy can see and hear them.

5. CHARGE!

Throw a spear right over the enemy's army. It pays honor to Odin, god of war, plus it will really unnerve your enemy.

FORM A SHIELD WALL

Form a shield wall so you push the enemy backward across the battlefield.

ABORT

If things are going badly, but your SHIELD WALL is still intact, you can carefully leave the fight. Move backward, and your enemy probably won't chase you—he'll be too tired.

MOVE FORWARD

In a SHIELD WALL it's always better to keep moving forward, no matter what's hurtling toward you.

HOLD YOUR NERVE!

When you are facing a CAVALRY CHARGE it's tempting to turn and run. If you do, enemy soldiers can easily throw a spear into your back. But if you hold firm, the horses will turn away at the last minute.

HERVOR'S GUIDE TO RAIDING

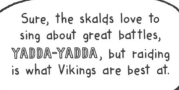

Sure, the skalds love to sing about great battles, YADDA-YADDA, but raiding is what Vikings are best at.

There are a bunch of different ways to go raiding, some more violent than others. Pick whatever method is appropriate for the situation—or floats your boat.

QUICK NICKING

Strandhogg is what Vikings call stealing stuff that they spot on the seashore, when no-one is watching. It's low-key, so you're unlikely to get hurt, but you won't get much more than a few cows or sheep.

YOINK!

BURNING DOWN THE HOUSE

House burning is often used in blood feuds at home, but it's also useful when raiding, especially when you have fewer warriors than whoever you're attacking.

Vikings wait until their victims are asleep at night, then set fire to the house they're sleeping in. Victims won't have time to arm themselves and will run out the front door one at a time, making them easy to catch or kill.

MONK-Y BUSINESS

Monasteries have huge treasure hoards—if you can get to them. If the monks see you coming, they will bury the treasure so you can't find it. Monks can also be sold as thralls.

Just remember not to burn down the buildings. That way, if you wait long enough new monks (with new treasure) will move in and you can raid the place again in a few years.

THE BOOTY

Finally, the good stuff. **THE PLUNDER. THE TREASURE. THE LOOT.** This is why Vikings risk their lives sailing to far-flung places: because if you don't plunder, you don't get paid.

1. TREASURE HUNTING

Find things made from gold or silver and you've hit the jackpot. Jewelry, coins and religious objects can be shared out and melted down to turn into arm rings.

ARM RINGS are a good way to carry around your loot, as no one can steal them without cutting off your arm—and not many people want to try cutting off a Viking's arm!

2. FAIR TRADE

Goods such as cloth, furs, wood and grain are harder to transport. Conveniently, merchants tend to follow Viking raiding parties at a safe distance, so you can easily sell your stolen items for cash.

3. SHARING IS CARING

Everything that gets looted on a raid, including treasure, goods and thralls, gets pooled together then shared evenly (only the leader gets a bigger share).

How are we dividing up this monk, then?

Apart from looting, there are other ways to milk your enemy for extra cash.

4. A HANDSOME RANSOM

Sometimes kidnapping people and precious objects and holding them for ransom can be more rewarding than simply stealing stuff. Important people get the best prices: one abbot in Frankia was ransomed for 686 pounds of gold, and 3,250 pounds of silver! This is more than you would get in a raid.

5. HOLY RELICS

Christians will also pay good money to get their holy relics back (bits of dry old bone that they think belonged to saints, and so have special powers).

Save the bones. You can get gold for them from the Christians.

6. TRIBUTE ACT

If you've just defeated your enemy in battle, it's a good opportunity to demand a tribute. This means they pay you a huge amount of money to go away. Even after the tribute cash is shared out, it can be enough to set up each Viking in the army for life. And even better, the local tax collectors go and get it for you. Pretty sweet.

TA-DA!!

$$

7. LAND OF PLENTY

Raiding might be exciting, but many Vikings are happy to settle down on a nice bit of land. Empty territory is easy to claim, but when conquering occupied countries, the best thing to do is simply kill all the leaders.

As long as you treat them no worse than their previous lord, the local peasants won't care who's in charge.

Your Brutalness.

BEHAVE LIKE PIRATES

Another way to make money is to make like a pirate and steal it. Merchant ships are the easiest targets and come packed full of goodies. But remember: the aim isn't to sink the ship. Ships are valuable! The idea is to capture them.

TAKE YOUR LARGEST SHIP
Larger ships have two big advantages: they can carry more loot and are harder for attackers to board.

WATCH OUT FOR COPYCATS

Watch out for the Wends! They launch pirate raids in ships that look just like Viking longships, so it can be easy to mistake Wends for fellow Vikings. The tell-tale sign is that Wends cut their hair close to the scalp.

ANCHOR YOURSELF

Use grappling hooks and anchors to fasten your ship to the one you want to loot. Where you go, they'll go.

81

VIKING HEALTHCARE

Being a Viking is a risky business and Viking armies don't have health and safety rules. If you get injured (which is highly likely) these are the sorts of treatments you can expect:

FIRST AID

For minor wounds, a layer of cobweb or plantain weed is laid over the cut. Make sure to remove the spiders from the web first, though.

Oh no! They're fighting again. I only just rebuilt this!

I can smell what I had for lunch.

That can't be good.

STOMACH WOUNDS

Serious stomach wounds are usually fatal. You can find out how bad your wound is by drinking strong-smelling leek broth. If your wound starts to smell of leek, it means your guts have been pierced and you'll die within three days.

BROKEN BONES

If the broken bone hasn't pierced the skin, the bone can be set by an expert (though this is painful). If the bone has pierced the skin, the best choice is to cut off the limb. However, this usually kills the patient.

> Would you prefer to die from your wounds or your treatment?

SEVERE BLEEDING

Bleeding is stopped by cauterizing (burning the wound with red-hot iron). If stitches are needed, holes are made in the flesh first with a metal spike. The wound is then sewn up with a bone needle.

SHOCK

The chaos and violence of combat can give some warriors "war fetter" (meaning "foot terror"). It causes them to wander around aimlessly, confused. Rest and peace and quiet is the best medicine.

SORRY YOU'RE DYING

GOOD LUCK

GET WELL SOON

THE SWORD'S SLEEP

> Ahh, my favorite part... death! Depending on how you die, you could end up in one of a number of Viking afterworlds.

VALHALLA

This is where every Viking wants to go, but you only get into Valhalla if you die in battle. After a battle, Odin sends down his Valkyries (ghostly battle-maidens) to collect the souls of those who die.

The Valkyries take the dead up to the great hall Valhalla, which is made of gold, with a roof of shields and mail coats. Everyone feasts and fights, until Ragnarok—the battle against the giants at the end of time. Epic!

SECOND BEST

If you were very good, you might get to go to a different hall, such as Brimir or Sindri. These are pleasant places where they serve good ale.

SNAKE FOOD

The souls of murderers and oath breakers go to the hellish Nástrandir, a hall made of woven snakes that drip with venom. The most wicked get thrown into a well and eaten by a giant snake.

NOWHERE

Unfortunately for them, most souls just hang around as ghosts in the graves where they are buried, with whatever their family buried them with.

SO, DO YOU REALLY WANT TO BE A VIKING?

You now know what it's like to be a Viking.

Is it a lifestyle you find to your liking?

IF WARRIOR LIFE APPEALS,
BUT YOU'RE NOT CONVINCED YOU'RE
THE VIKING TYPE, TURN TO PAGE 96
FOR OTHER ANCIENT JOB OPTIONS!

VIKING WORLD MAP

Where would you like to raid?

ICELAND
REYKJAVIK

FAROE
ISLANDS

SCOTLAND

NORTH
SEA

WESTERN OCEAN

IRELAND
CORK   DUBLIN

YORK
(JORVIK)

ENGLAND
LONDON

SCALE
310 miles

Viking routes

FLANDERS

ROUEN

PARIS

LEON

FRANKIA

LISBON

SPAIN

CORDOBA

SEVILLE

STRAITS
OF GIBRALTAR
(Narrows of Narvesund)

MIDDLE SEA

88

NORWAY

SWEDEN

FINLAND

BIRKA

BALTIC SEA
(Eastern Sea)

HOLMGARD

ESTLAND

STARAYA LADOGA
(ALDEIGJUBORG)

GARDARIKI

UPPAKRA

HEDEBY

WENDLAND

KIEV
(KOENUGARD)

...NI
...UNA)

ROME

GREEK EMPIRE

CONSTANTINOPLE
(MIKLIGARD)

BLACK SEA

89

GLOSSARY

ABBEY a large community of monks or nuns

BERSERKER a Viking warrior who can work himself into an uncontrollable rage

BLOOD FEUD a lengthy fight between two families, where each group kills members of the other group in revenge over a long period of time

BROADAXE a very large axe held with two hands

CAMPAIGN a planned battle, or series of battles, that has a clear goal such as invading or looting another country

DRAKKAR a large Viking warship

DUEL a pre-arranged fight between two people to settle an argument (often to the death)

FORTIFICATION reinforcements on a building to protect against attack

FRANKIA the kingdom of France

GARDARIKI modern-day Russia

GREEK FIRE a chemical that burns and can be catapulted or poured onto enemy ships to set them on fire

HANDAXE a small axe held with one hand

JARL a lord in Norse society, the rank below king

MIKLIGARD modern-day Istanbul

MONASTERY a place where monks live together

MONK a member of a religious group of men who promise to stay poor, worship God every day, and not get married

MOORS people from North Africa who also settled in Spain after 711 CE

NASTRANDIR the Viking afterlife for murderers and oathbreakers, it is a hall made of snakes where a giant snake chews on especially bad people's corpses

NORSEMEN the people who lived in Scandinavia (including Vikings)

ODIN the chief god in the Norse belief system

OUTLAW a criminal who is not allowed to be part of society anymore

PEASANT a poor farmer

PLUNDER to steal things, usually using violence

RAID a sudden attack, often with the purpose of stealing things

RELIC in Christianity this is a bone or other body part of a holy person, or an object that they touched

RUNES the letters used in words by the Norse people

SEERESS a woman who can see into the future

SHIELD-MAIDEN a female warrior

SIEGE when a town or city is surrounded by an army to cut off supplies such as food and water

SKALD a poet who composes songs about the king or jarl

SNEKKE a long and shallow Viking warship

STANDARD a flag flown in battle

STRANDHOGG hit-and-run raiding along a coastline

SUN STONE a crystal used
to find the location of the Sun
in cloudy weather

RUS the people of Scandinavian
origin who lived in Russia

THRALL someone who is captured in
a raid and treated as property

TRIBUTE a payment made by
a country or a ruler to a foreign
force as the price of peace or
protection

VALHALLA The Norse god Odin's
hall. Viking warriors who died in
battle go there after death

VALKYRIE ghostly female warriors
who live with Odin in Valhalla

VARANGIAN GUARD the Byzantine
emperor Basil's elite bodyguard of
Viking warriors

READING RUNES

Need to write a letter to another Viking? Then you need to learn to write runes. The runic alphabet varies a little bit depending on exactly where in Scandinavia you are, but this is the Norwegian version.

RUNE

MAKES THE SOUND

f/v   u/w/o/y   th   a   r   k/g   h   n

i/e   a   s   t/d   b/p   m   l   R

The letters are made of straight lines, making them easy to inscribe into stone.

INDEX

abbeys 56, 90
archery 23, 61
armour 32–33, 39, 49, 70
axes 7, 19, 22, 29, 87, 90

battle 10, 21–23, 27–29, 31, 34,
36–37, 48, 53, 58, 64–66, 68,
70, 74, 79, 84, 90–92
battleaxes 29
battlefields 68, 70, 72
battle techniques 34
berserkers 48–49, 64, 71, 90
blood feud 15, 75, 90
bows 29, 51
Brimir 85
broadaxes 29, 90

campaigns 28, 52, 58–59, 90
Canada 6, 40
cavalry charge 73
commanders 64, 69

defense force 23
Denmark 41
drakkars 36–37, 90

enemy 27, 29, 34–35, 49–50,
63, 65, 68, 70–73, 78,–79, 90
England 17–18, 41, 52, 88

figureheads 37, 43
Finland 43, 51, 89
folklore 35
forts 35, 60
Frankia 55,–56, 78, 88, 90
furs 11, 51, 56, 77

Gardariki 56, 89–90
Greek Empire 89
Greek fire 57, 90

handaxes 29, 90
healthcare 82
helmets 20, 32–33
horns 33
horses 44–45, 61–62, 69, 73

Ireland 17, 53, 88

jarls 13, 24–25, 37, 61, 90–91

kings 5, 12–13, 19, 24–25, 37,
52, 56, 61, 90–91

longships 18, 20, 36–37, 65, 81
loot 40, 47, 60–61, 63, 76,
80–81

magic 31, 43, 51

mail shirts 32–33, 84
Mediterranean 17,55
merchant ships 80
Mikligard 46, 57, 89–90
monasteries 53, 75, 90
monks 75, 77, 90
Moors 55, 91

Nastrandir 85, 91
Norway 19, 89

oarsmen 37–38
Odin 35, 48, 72, 84, 91–92

peasants 18, 60, 79, 91
pirates 47, 80–81

Ragnarok 84
raids 13–15, 17–20, 28, 38,
44–45, 47, 50, 54, 56–58,
74–75, 77–79, 88,
runes 31, 43, 91, 93

sagas 5, 14
Scandinavia 5–6, 12, 17, 36, 42,
91–93
sea battles 37
seeresses 58, 91
shield-maidens 5, 14, 87, 91
shields 34–35, 48, 67, 71–73
shield-burgs 35

shield walls 34–35, 67, 72–73
shipwrecks 42–43
siege 29, 91
Sindri 85
skalds 5, 10, 16, 19, 28, 61, 66,
74, 91
ski-Finns 51
snekkes 36–38, 91
Spain 55, 88, 91
spears 28, 32, 66, 72–73
swords 14, 20, 22, 29–32, 84
standard bearers 68
Strandhogg 38, 74, 91
sun stones 35
swine-wedges 35
sword's sleep, the 84

thralls 15, 19, 53, 57, 75, 92
tributes 79, 92

Valhalla 84, 92
Valkyries 84, 92
Varangian guard 46–47, 57, 92
Viking army 12, 20–21, 24, 62

weapons 13, 15, 22, 28–30, 39,
53, 57
warships 38, 90–91
Wendland 54, 89
Wends 54, 81
witches 51

I personally can't understand why anyone wouldn't want to be a **VIKING**. But if it really doesn't float your boat, you could try being a **ROMAN SOLDIER**, I suppose.